Killstreme

More by Rayne:

Collecting Rayne Vol 2

(the next collection of stories, including:)

The Other Place

Boys Will Be Boys

Tantalize

Daddy Issues

Necrosis

Collecting Rayne Vol 1

(a collection of stories, including:)

My Christmas Story

Degenerate

The Boy

Devour

Retaliation

XXX

app

The Embalmer

Killstreme

by Rayne Havok

This is a work of fiction, if you find any similarities what-so- ever they are coincidental.

No part of this book may be copied or reproduced without prior authorization from the author.

WARNING:

MAY OFFEND

one

"Mommy, can I have just one more story?"

"Oh, you think you need another one? My little pip squeak isn't sleepy yet?" I kiss Addi on her sweet, freshly shampooed, head. I hate to leave her; I really do, especially at night. It became a necessity after her dad left, leaving us to the wolves, it was this or let the world continue to fuck me.

We are lucky to have my mom so close, having her here to keep Addi safe while I'm gone is more help than she will ever know. Having someone trustworthy, in a world full of creeps, and bad guys hunting for innocence, makes working possible.

"Ok, one more, but you have to read it. Show me you're a big girl ready for school in a few months." Her eyes grow large, she is so excited to have a teacher. It makes her feel grown up.

"Ok, I'll read. She hops off the bed, and just like always, she grabs a big book off the shelf, tonight her selection is Harry Potter. Plopping down, she flips the book open to a random page and runs her finger along the words as she speaks.

I turn the book right-side-up, which doesn't interrupt her at all, she isn't reading anyway.

"And then, Harry does magic. And he is so happy. And his mommy doesn't have to go to work. And he is in love. And Harry is soooo strong."

I lie back against her head-board and try not to laugh as she excitedly builds the story in short bursts. She flips the pages quickly, and within a few minutes, we have finished the book.

"That's quite a journey Harry took us on tonight, isn't it?" Taking the book from her lap, I replace it on the shelf and give her one more kiss, savoring her. I'll be back before she wakes, but I'll still miss her all the same.

"Yea, it was good. I'm gonna have good dreams now."

"Goodnight, pip. I love you *way* more than you love me."

"That's impastabowl, mommy."

Leaving the spinning unicorn nightlight on, I close the door until there is only a crack through which I watch her settle in, and then close her eyes. Her lips turn up in a small smile as, I can only assume, she replays Harry's adventures.

"Honey, I have everything under control," my mom starts her reassurances as I enter the room.

I know she can tell I don't like leaving Addi, nor do I prefer these hours, but I have to make it on my own, and this is what pays. "I know mom, I appreciate you. I'll be back before you guys wake up."

Heading for the door, I blow her a kiss and then leave as quietly as I can. I don't have enough time for another story if Addi gets out of bed tonight.

***

The man brandishes a huge knife, a machete, maybe. I don't know the difference. I just know that I like what he does with it. This film is one of my favorites. She's about to get bloody.

I reach down and tug on my dick, I know the timing perfectly, and I want to come to the masked-man fucking one of her stab wounds. It only lasts a minute before he comes, and then hacks the back of her neck, so, I need to get that sweet spot where we finish together.

The blonde is screaming inside her mask. The only things visible are her red lips and pleading eyes, begging him to show compassion and to leave her alone. But I know he doesn't. I know everything this man does to her as if it were my own experience.

The moment comes, and I let go, coming hard just as I see his bloody dick pull out of her side. I clean myself up while I finish the rest, watching the final wound spurt and her body fall still. The man walks over to the tripod and switches off the camera. His face obscured by a bloody mask, leaving only his eyes visible. They are excited, wild, and are exactly what I assume the eyes of a killer would be.

Catching my breath, but leaving my pants around my ankles, I sign in and look for any new uploads. If I do this before I get off, I'm afraid I'll be too turned on to look for warning signs, or traps, from authorities looking to make a bust on the dark web.

I can't help that I love this stuff, it's the only thing I can get off to anymore.

The gorier, the better. The more I see a woman beg, the harder I get. The blood pouring out, drying on her skin. I imagine the smell of copper mingling with the scent of their pussies. The sticky sound it makes while fucking them covered in blood is better than any soundtrack imaginable.

After a cursory glance, nothing stands out as being new. This category isn't as popular as some of the others. I mean, if I wanted tiny-teens-being-fucked-by-big-black-cock, I'd have something new every day. But snuff can't be produced on a bus driving around college towns and spammed across the internet. It can be years before something fresh makes it into the scene. Which is why I know my collection like the top side of my cock.

I see that a few of the regulars are online and open a chat with BinKilinU.

'anything new?'

'you would be the first to know.'

'thanks anyway'

I close the window, change my VPN location, and look down at my flaccid dick. I was really hoping for something fresh, but it doesn't look like it's going to happen.

I shut down the desktop and head upstairs.

"Wesley?"

"Yea, babe, it's me." Undressing, I climb in bed with her, tucking my arms under my head, keeping my eyes trained on the ceiling.

Stephanie snuggles in, even though she knows it just makes me too hot and unable to sleep.

Her hand takes hold of my dick and I practically roll my eyes. It hasn't gotten up from her efforts in a very long time. She mostly blames herself, and fuck, it might be something she's doing. It's not likely, but it only encourages her to work harder, which, in turn, makes her stress out more when she can't get me up, or off. And then, she doesn't do anything well. It's like watching her trying to jack-off a garden hose.

"I want you inside of me, I miss having this big dick fill me up."

"I know you do, Steph," I sound remorseful. And a small part of me wishes I *could* perform, but nothing is as exhilarating as snuff, even simply watching it, has a more gratifying finish than with her.

"I'm so horny, Wes, I just need this." Before she jumps into the conversation about seeing a doctor for erection pills one more time. I roll over and spread her legs, reaching into her nightstand for the big rubber dildo. Spitting on the tip, I jam it into her. She arches her back and I fuck her hard. Sucking her clit into my mouth, I get her off quickly as she comes all over, creaming down my arm. I give her a few more deep plunges of the thick, neon, dildo and then she's had her fill.

Not even a twitch from my dick. I used to get hard as a rock at the sight of a juicy pussy. Since setting my eyes on that short film—leaving a woman covered in death and a massive cream pie oozing from her lifeless pussy— I've been immune to the mundane and typical. That four minutes was all it took to create my affliction.

I let her clean herself up and I throw a towel on the wet spot, rolling over so she doesn't get too close.

"Thanks, babe," she says, finally able to rest.

I close my eyes, but sleep doesn't come. Her heavy breathing keeps me alert. The annoying taste in my mouth I want to swish out, but don't want to disturb her, left lingering on my tongue until it sours and I can no longer stand it.

Creeping out of bed, I head down the stairs to get a drink, avoiding the steps that make creaking noises. I catch a glimpse of the monitor out of the corner of my eye, my dick twitches like a junky needing a fix.

Fucking thing.

It sure would be nice to get off inside a pussy again... maybe I could have her cos-play a computer monitor.

Just asking my wife to fuck me while I watch snuff is unimaginable, and not even in the realm of possibilities. If she were blind and deaf, I still couldn't risk my freedom for it. So, the screen, and my hand, are what I have.

Like a dutiful addict, I boot everything up and log on, fulfilling my cock's need.

Typing in a password that no one could guess if given endless attempts. I've set it to three tries before it overwrites my hard drive. I've never needed that many, luckily. It mostly takes one, knowing what's at stake.

Stephanie wouldn't know what to do with my setup if she were suddenly inclined to become a snoop. I was pretty paranoid when I set it that way, losing access would ruin what sex life I have. I take my time entering the letter and numerical code, getting it right on the first attempt, the screen comes to life.

My pulse quickens and my cock jumps when I see that I have a DM. It's from BinKilinU and I can't open it fast enough. I'm disappointed when I don't see a file to download. There is just a single word on the page that says *'application'*. BinKilinU has never been one to disappoint, or give pause, so I click away.

The loaded page opens with a heading *'Killstreme—a snuff production company'*, followed by a series of questions about me and what I'm in to. As I read through a few inquiries, I realize that I am being asked to apply for an opportunity to star in a snuff film of my own. My cock is achingly hard and dribbling down my thigh as a response.

My heart is pounding out of my chest as I try to gather myself to answer the questions. They're asking why I think I would be a good leading man.

If I could do this, be a real snuffer, my whole life would be perfect. I'd likely never have to risk signing on here again. I could have a copy of myself taking a life while fucking the last breath from her naked, mutilated body.

All the fantasies montage through my head, making it impossible to keep track of reality.

The anticipation has my hands shaking. This might be the most excited I have ever been. Scratch that, this is, *bar none*, the most exhilarated I have ever felt.

Trying to both type, and satiate my dick, is impossible. I put my efforts into getting off so I can return my focus to the application. The prospect of this has me feeling more teenager than I had when I was actually that age.

Gripping my balls hard and wrapping my hand around the base of my cock, I stroke myself to the image of a girl in my head. Her mangled body going limp beneath me just as the ribbons of hot come ooze over my clenched knuckles, sweat beading on my brow.

I return to the form without wasting even a second to clean up, just wiping the mess on my shorts.

The first question stumps me, I wonder if my real name is a good idea.

Fuck it.

Wesley—no need for a last name.

A bunch of other personal information, and then the fun part. It's asking what I'd like to do with the subject— their word, not mine. I'm thinking of all the things that I'd like to have in my personal video. Both from what I've seen, and what I've fantasized in my mind. And I list them all.

I want to fuck her raw.

I want to make her insides bleed.

I want to cut her and sever her limbs.

I want to come inside her wounds.

I would love to put on a show, porn level come and snuff level blood. I'm strong and big, and will definitely be able to make this film legendary. I'm not squeamish or inhibited in any way.

I reread my answers and make sure that they understand I'd really be a good fit for the role, and then I send it off, crossing my fingers that it's not a sting. I actually think it would be worth serving the time for the off chance that this might be real.

Oh, my fucking *god*, I hope it's real.

I lean back against the leather chair, thinking how cruel I could actually be to another human. I try to think it might be horrible, that it would do something to my soul. But I'm kidding myself. I am all fucking in.

A small chime from the speaker indicates I have a new message.

My heart jumps when I see the subject line—'application approved'. Upon clicking, my screen is filled with photos of women, below a heading that reads: 'Make your selection'.

Excitement makes it hard to focus on any one of them in particular, each of their faces blur into the next as adrenaline courses through my body, dilating my pupils.

I have to try hard to calm myself so I can choose wisely, I need one I will not regret. This girl is going to be mine forever, I better not fuck this up.

The photos are close ups of their faces, and then a shot of their bodies, both clothed and naked. Lastly, pussies—shaved and not, some of the biggest bubble gum lips I've ever seen, and I can imagine taking a bite.

Oh, fuck.

I force my attention away from their naughty bits, and remind myself the importance of the *whole* package. There are all types—natural, enhanced, tall, short, thin, fat, black, white, (and everything in between) ranging in age from college freshman to mature cougar. I feel like a kid in a candy store with a stolen credit card. Unlimited choices, making it nearly impossible to select.

I wonder how they have access to all these women.

How are they kept?

No matter, there is one I keep coming back to. Her shoulder length copper hair and huge emerald eyes make her seem sweet and wholesome. The naked shots of her make me feel that long lost tingle.

I'd love to ruin that sweetness.

I check-mark the box beneath her portfolio.

Another screen pops up and lists a day and time on an appointment card. An address is shown only after I select the 'ok' button. It is across town, in the industrial district. I've never been there, but I recognize the zip code. It's just about a two-hour drive to get there.

I'll have to make a cover story for Stephanie, let her know I'll be doing something for work. I don't usually have anything to do outside of business hours, which are spent at home in this office, but I can't have her asking to tag along.

It's tomorrow, 9pm. Less than 24 hours and I'm going to be the star of my very own snuff. I wonder for a moment if they will pay me, then quickly laugh off the thought—I would actually pay *them*, gladly.

It's 2am when I finally switch off the computer, knowing I won't be able to sleep, especially if Stephanie gets cuddly. The thought of her thick, hot body pressed against me instead of the girl in the photo repulses me.

Images of the small red head's puffy nipples, set dead center on perky tits, resting high above her tiny waist, flared hips, round ass, all running free through my mind.

Her blush colored pussy stands out like a target, surrounded by her pale skin, lightly sprinkled with freckles. I can't help but think of all of the things I have wanted to do to a woman's body if given free reign, unbridled by consequence.

She is a tight little package that practically screams 'use me' and it's making it impossible to go upstairs to my own wife, who will now seem like a troll.

I decide to schedule an appointment online to have my junk waxed. I don't do it on the regular, but it makes my big dick look even bigger, gives me a bit more sensation.

After 10am, I'll be clean as a whistle and ready for my show. I decide to abstain from jacking off until my snuff debut. I can come multiple times, but the loads are bigger, and far more impressive, if there is some wait-time before hand. I want as many epic come shots as possible.

I lay on the sofa, body tingling with excitement while my cock throbs with anticipation, making it a challenge to get some rest before the best day of my life happens.

two

Two hours and nineteen minutes of driving later, I pull into an empty lot that my phone promised is my destination. I park in darkness, with extra effort to be sure that it is done legally. I can't be tied to this place via a ticket because of a stupid mistake.

That's how they catch amateurs.

Before I get out, I take thorough look around for anything suspicious—a masked man, ready to rob me. Strangers of any sort, looking for trouble—anything amiss. The coast seems clear, so I gather myself and open the door. The area is quiet and still, the only sounds are crickets and my own shuffling feet.

Two large industrial buildings obscure the view of a smaller one sandwiched between. There is only one door visible from the lot, as I continue to the smaller brick building that bears the numbers indicated in the address.

I assumed that there was going to be a person to greet me, so I'm surprised when the door is not only unlocked, but right inside it is the girl—*my girl*.

The door closes heavily behind me as I stand for a second to take in my surroundings. The copper haired girl is laying, sprawled out, on an old mattress covered in a white sheet, at the end of the well-lit room.

She is wearing a mask, covering only the top of her face, her open eyes locking with mine, nervously watching me between her frantic blinking.

My eye catches a note stuck to the wall, addressed to me with a list of instructions. *'Wesley, please enjoy. If you'd like to keep your anonymity, there is a mask on the table, the choice is yours.'*

I slip on the face covering, very much like hers, just enough fabric to disguise features, but not so much that it feels claustrophobic.

The instructions tell me to undress, which I do, and to be mindful of camera angles. Of which, there are two on tripods for the back view, one mounted on the wall, just above her head, and several along the ceiling on either side. Too many to count, let alone mind. But I will do my best, and hopefully they will have enough to edit a good film for me—and I suppose, anyone who is lucky enough to receive a copy of my work. I smile at the thought of being the envy of so many men.

Jealous, and dreaming, of being the lucky guy in the lenses' view. Luck has never really been on my side, and I'm beyond grateful for the turn of the tide.

There is a rolling table in the corner adjacent to the mattress that I'm drawn to. As I walk toward it, the girl starts kicking against her ankle restraints.

"Hey," her soft voice stops me. I hadn't expected conversation. I didn't know *what* to expect.

Ignoring her whining, I notice the table is topped with all the things I said I would like to use for her execution. The machete, and a few other sharp objects. A metal pipe that makes my dick twitch, chains, ball-gag, dildos—*huge* dildos, butt plugs, scissors, each item looking shiny and new.

My mouth salivates, and my cock quickly hardens to be ready for its role as my co-star.

I feel compelled to use every single thing on the table, and can only hope there isn't a time limit that will prevent me from doing so. I just have to keep her alive until I've had enough. Theoretically, I could make this last a *long* fucking time—if I'm careful.

I move the table closer to the mattress, her little piggy squeals become more frantic. I see the reason for the ball gag, but I like it more when I can hear that agony and fear in the cries for mercy. It feels secluded enough that I can afford that luxury.

Running my hand up her leg, her body freezes, panic alters the shape of her eyes. I give her one warning, not to move or she will be sorry, that she chooses not to heed.

The vise grip pliers from the table are calling out to me, I've got to show her who's in charge here, and that I don't care how much she begs.

Gripping her foot in my hand. The teeth of the pliers squeeze down on the nail of her big toe as the vice grip locks. I watch her face lose all color, draining the last bit of hope from her heart.

An ear-piercing scream tears loose of her throat as I slowly twist and pull on her hot pink nail, ripping it away from the skin underneath.

Her body begins to tremble, terror is winning. Her shaky breath is loud, beautiful tears stream down her face.

My hand instinctively reaches for my cock, trying to quell the ache. Her eyes drop to my sudden movement, her lips snarl before she calls me a sick fuck.

She has no fucking idea.

Taking her foot to examine it, watching the blood drip freely, I lick and then suck it into my mouth painfully hard, she gags as though she might vomit.

When she realizes it's too difficult to watch, she closes her eyes and sobs. Tears roll down her face. Her chest trembles with her cries. She is fucking beautiful like this—I have absolutely made the right choice.

Her, sad, emerald eyes, filled with terror, pleading with mine to be her savior. My own, hooded with the burning desire to watch her bleed, creasing at the corners with my slowly growing smirk, are not giving her what she needs. I'm not her salvation—I'm her demise.

I massage my cock until it's full, and then climb on top of her and in between her legs. She's so small, I must feel massive to her.

I push my throbbing cock inside of her, the pressure of her tight pussy eases some of the ache, bringing a focus I hadn't been able to gain since walking in here. Wrapping my hand around her throat, leaning into her face, I lick the tears from her cheeks and then taste her lips, her fruity chap-stick mingles with the salt in a delectable way.

I can feel the fear in her rapid pulse as my cock pounds into her deeply, hard enough to shove her head against the wall repeatedly with each thrust.

I keep her air restricted at her throat. Reaching with my fingers, I force them into her mouth and pull it open with her bottom jaw. A few more hard thrusts into her exquisite hole and my cock is begging for release.

Moving upward to my target, I unload into her mouth, milking every drop of my load, and watching it pool in the back of her throat.

My dick is still achingly hard, but becomes insufferable when she has no choice but to swallow my come in order to breathe. The overflow dribbling down her cheeks and chin.

Returning to my position between her legs, my attention switches to her nipples, ever hard, and kind of big for her small tits. I suck each one deep enough to redden. I can feel her heart thudding in her chest as I bite her tummy, not enough to draw blood, but definitely leaving a dental impression.

I release the tether holding her feet to the footboard and fold her in half, moving her ankles next to her wrists at the headboard and then reattach the belt-like strap, giving me complete access to her puffy pussy lips and tight little asshole.

I take a second to admire what she has to offer, breathing her aroma deep into my lungs before I suck as much of her pale, bare, flesh into my mouth as I can manage.

Her taste evokes everything I crave, youth, desire, ownership and a sweet agony that causes my skin to erupt in excitement. She squirms, and begs, but the pain in her toe hopefully reminds her that resistance is futile—and dangerous.

I nip her harder, relishing the flavor of her fear, and sweetness of her submission, licking it from my lips, savoring it for my memory.

"Do you know why you're here?" I ask her, watching her eyes well with tears between the blinks that send them streaming down her cheeks.

"Please, just leave me alone," she says with a trembling chin.

"I will not be doing that. I'm here to make a movie," I taunt her, helping her realize that there is no amount of pleading that will save her.

"Don't hurt me anymore, I'll do whatever you want me to, I'll be good, I promise."

"It will stop hurting when I've had my fill, but that won't be until you're dead." An involuntary smile reaches my eyes when I say the words to her. I can feel the moment it hits her, the flood of heat rushing from her core.

I press my thumb against her puckered asshole, keeping my eyes on hers for a moment to watch her reaction.

My thumb breaks through, forcing into her tight, perfectly shaped, classic example of anatomy. Hefting her ass up, I rest it on top of my thighs, aligning it with my cock before I shove into her remorselessly. She clenches tightly but it's too late, I'm in too deep, and she can't prevent me from entering as I use my weight to force inside. She screams and bucks, only helping me to penetrate her completely.

It's tight—virgin tight, and feels so good, letting myself succumb to the bliss, my eyes rolling back in my head as I glide in and out of her, slowly, making her feel every inch of me while I lose myself in the pleasure of it all.

A sudden shift in the room, something I can't identify, brings my eyes open in a beat. A sting in my neck, sharp and surprising, forces a confused and startled yelp from my mouth.

And then there is only black.

A pounding in my head rouses me, a thundering pain in my extremities reminds me something isn't right. One second, I am inside a dream come true, the next, I'm waking up.

I survey what happened while I was out, and maybe a reason for it. I realize I'm in some sort of contraption, hoisting me above the mattress. Securing me by my midsection, like some superman imposter, leaving my arms and legs to dangle. I assume that's what the sharp pins and needles feeling is coming from. They are asleep.

It couldn't have been too long though, as I'm redirected to the girl on the bed, being unshackled by two women—both naked and in masks of their own.

They've broken loose and are helping free the others?

Does that even make sense?

What the fuck is going on?

She is loose now, rubbing each of her wrists, and then daring a look at her toe.

"What the fuck? Why did you guys take so long? Look what he did to my fucking toe!" she yells, frantically climbing off the mattress that was supposed to be the stage for my performance of a lifetime.

My state of shock is not helping me understand anything, I need help deciphering what the hell is going on here.

I'm not able to dwell in the confusion for long. The soft voice of one of the women comes from behind me. I can't turn to see her, although I wish I could, the harness around my middle keeps me immobile.

"Yea, I'm sorry about your nail. I've already sent a message to our Dr. friend; she is expecting you when we are done here. And we know how much you enjoy the rough stuff; you aren't fooling anyone. It probably made you come. It's not like we were going to let him kill you. After a good pedicure, you'll be fine"

"Listen, ladies, you got this all wrong." I try very hard to sound like I'm not about to become shrill and shit myself from fear.

The copper haired girl speaks instead. "We don't have anything wrong, *Wesley*," saying my name as snidely as I've ever heard it, she grins. "We have

everything exactly the way we intended... well almost."
Bringing attention to her toe with an irritated chuff.

As if the words spoken were their cue, all three
converge on me. My arms fight to grab them, my legs
kick, but to no avail, I'm quickly left too tired to expend
any more energy.

They've stayed far enough away for me to miss every
blow, watching, as if waiting for me to gas out, getting to
work only after I still. I struggle mentally to regain my
strength for a possible surprise attack later.

I realize quickly that chance may never come, when I
lurch up, the harness tipping, and I'm in a standing
position without being able to touch the ground.

The dark-haired woman, with the Betty Paige
haircut steps forward, and even in this warped time, my
dick takes notice of the colorful tattoos that cover most
of her tight body.

She moves behind me, lightly running her hands up my back, which I think for a moment could be ok—that I may have gotten the wrong idea about the situation—but then, she pinches a chunk of skin at my shoulder blade area hard enough to make me flinch. A sharp stab bites, letting me know that this whole movie thing was not for me, that I may be the star in this film in a very different way. It causes my heart to sink as the roles are reversed.

I should've known. I've never been lucky.

The other shoulder gets the same treatment. I can feel the blood trickle from those areas. Panic turns to hysteria—an even higher-level claws it's way in when a jerking tug hefts my shoulders up. A yelp lodges in my throat.

The last girl, the petite, naked, blonde, with youthful pigtails and doe eyes a shade of lavender I've never seen before, comes to my front and releases the harness from my middle. I remain suspended by the hooks in my shoulders.

Her barbie doll body presses against me. I try to shake her loose, but I have no real plan. What the fuck could I possibly do now? I think hard about my options. Pleading is never going to work—these don't seem like amateurs, and this doesn't seem like an accident.

They've brought me here under the guise of satisfying my sickest fantasy, and I fucking fell for it like a jack ass. I mentally chastise myself.

Escaping the hooks suspending me from the ceiling is a no-go.

How did I miss those?

How did I miss the rig that caught me in the first place? —may be a better question.

I look to the ceiling for the answers that don't come. The room was built for this trap.

It dawns on me... why the fuck would this girl let me do all that stuff to her in the first place? They could have just locked me up before it had even gotten this far. What the fuck kind of sick twisted games are these bitches in to?

The ginger girl's ass has got to be torn from what I did to it with no lube—and she played the victim so fucking well.

Who the fuck are these women?

"What if I had started with the really sharp stuff?" I blurt out, honestly wondering about it, and also trying to buy some time to think more about my escape.

"*Please*, you guys are all the same—so excited to fuck—instant gratification is your genders downfall. If you *had* gone too far too quickly, my girls would have jumped in. A toe nail is nothing, Brin had half of her pinky lopped off by one of you fuckers our first year. We don't fuck around anymore. Now shut up," she says to me. Then, addressing her raven-haired friend, who is holding up said pinky in a way that declares she's proud of it, she says, "Brin, why don't you get Wesley's ass hooks in place. He looks like he's ready to play now."

"I don't want to play," I whimper, sounding pathetic and juvenile.

The tattooed girl gets to work, looking a little too excited to be tasked with something so horrible. I feel the familiar pinch at the top of my ass cheek, and then, what I've come to know as the hook being inserted. A burning fire deep in the chunk of flesh at my hip lights up. The barbie girl is quick to give her friend help with the other side.

They rotate me into position and I'm back to facing the mattress, arms and legs hanging, but my midsection is up.

The piercing hooks aren't hurting anymore. I've seen suspension videos before and always thought it looked so painful, but after the initial burn that feels like a searing fire, it numbs quickly.

Brin, the tattooed girl, smacks Fiona on the ass. "You're up, copper top, make it a good one."

"The subscribers are gonna love this," Fiona says to her.

I roll my eyes, "I don't think a bunch of men are going to want to see you hurt me, if that's your angle, it's a shit one," I say, hoping I can grab at something that might give them pause.

"Oh," the blonde laughs high-pitched and wildly claps her hands, "this fucker thinks our viewers are men!" To me, she says, "honey, we have just shy of a million subscribers—all women. I think we know what tantalizes our audience."

"What the fuck?" I say, not loud enough to be heard and I'm not expecting a response.

How the fuck does that even happen? Women don't *like* this shit; they don't *need* this. It astonishes me that there are *three* women into this, let alone a whole underground group of bitches that *subscribe* to this sort of stream.

There really is some crazy shit out there in the world. It's scary how fucking unassuming they look. All three of these women are the type you'd see in the grocery store, shopping for their families, not kidnapping and torturing men. Over a million subscribers...there are so many, they can't all be here for gruesome acts of violence and blood, this has to be some hardcore dominatrix type shit and not the most extreme stream, this is something I can survive.

The two girls walk behind me, but I can't take my eyes from Fiona. I nearly swallow hard enough to chase my tonsils to my stomach when she gets on all fours under me, aiming her pussy right at me. Needless to say, I'm confused.

Turning her head to look at me, she says, "what was that you said about fucking me raw? Wanting my pussy to bleed." She wiggles her ass, "it doesn't *feel* raw, maybe you need to try harder."

I nearly laugh—my dick is never going to comply with her. I guess that's why I never thought something like this could happen to men. Whether it be with women behind the wheel, or not. You can't force a man hard, especially when he's nearly pissing himself.

My cock would never cooperate with her—or me, even if I really wanted this. "Good luck with that. I can't imagine you think I could actually get hard right now." I'm surprised I'm able to reach the level of sarcasm that I do in the state I'm in. It all feels like a waste of time.

"Oh, I came up with an idea for that, it's so good, I practically copyrighted it. It works wonders—and the subs love it." There's a glee in her eyes that stops my heart, this is a sick bitch.

I think for a minute she means submissives, but it doesn't look like this group is leaning that way. Which is weird, I've always thought it was the norm—that women loved to please and be dominated. And most importantly, I kinda thought they were nurturers not torturers. Wicked trickery is what all this is. My whole life is a lie.

Keeping my eyes diverted from hers calms me a little. I've seen excitement in the eyes of children at Christmas, and considers that to be the epitome of the word. This freak looks ready to come right now, just thinking about what horrible things she's planning to do.

"Ladies, as requested, we have our dad bod here." Brin is talking the way girls do when they're trying to be cute, and I assume it's for her subs.

"This boy wanted to *kill* Fiona. Can you fucking *believe* it? We found him on the dark web, sniffing around for some snuff," a pause, and then, "that's right, he *is* about to regret that." Brin laughs, and then they all laugh. "Fiona wants to use her special technique to get him big and hard for her."

Looking dead at me, Brin says, "Wes, they *love* it. Looks like you're going to be able to fuck Fiona like you've always dreamed."

"Yes, ladies," she continues her announcement with her eyes still on me, "we will *definitely* sock this sick fuck."

Fiona says something, drawing my attention away from Brin, "I am the inventor the sock." She winks, poking her tongue to her top lip. A look I would want to see at the far end of a bar, not right now, never right now. I have to look away.

The blonde girl comes forward with a small bag, setting it on the table.

Brin turns her focus to the ladies online. I'm hoping against everything, that they will talk her out of this, but she keeps laughing, and I don't think that's the mood everyone is in.

"Bella, glad you're here!" she shouts at the screen. "This guy bought one of your films, it's forty-grand-guy!"

That rings a bell. *I* paid forty-grand for one of the videos I have. It's my prized possession. I used one of my annual bonuses for it—the entire thing. I'd told Steph the company fucked me over. I had to talk her out of making me quit. It was a horrible time for our marriage, and one that only seemed worth it when I was reminded of what the money bought.

Brin brings the laptop over to me, and I'm face to face with the living, breathing, petite girl from my favorite film—my forty-grand film—as expected, and dreaded, my stomach drops.

I'm a fucking idiot.

It had all looked so real, the hole in her side, the massive things inserted *into* her, stretching her open. Gaping her ass wide enough to give birth out of it.

It's like seeing a ghost, here she is now, nerdy glasses surrounding the eyes I've come to countless times as they looked to have lost the vibrance of life—laughing at me now with a twinkle.

"Hey, Wes, thanks for the check. My son goes to private school now, and I got these babies." She lifts her top and shows her new giant boobs. I can't help but hope I get another chance to see them.

"You're welcome," I say, sarcastically. It makes her laugh.

Brin sets the laptop on the metal table, covering the implements on its top. She angles it up so that my image fills the screen, bringing to light my situation once again.

"Casey, Brin, get that dick ready for me," Fiona says, sounding oddly excited.

All the times I'd fantasized about hearing those words, two hot chicks ordered to fluff me... and *this* is how it happens. Just my luck. The coveted words don't bring my heart-rate up in anticipation of pleasure, instead, my unease skyrockets.

I feel hands on me immediately, but not on my dick, like I expect—where I think it should happen, no, they are at my asshole. A cool instrument is inserted with little finesse and I am reaching upward to new levels of terror. Then I feel it stretching and opening me—and I am launched to a whole new kind of fear throughout my body, I shudder.

"Speculum is in, moving on to the larger stretcher," I hear one of them say, in a tone befitting a medical assistant in a legit procedure.

"I'm so excited for this," Fiona, the fucking freak, says. Her hand comes up between her legs and she smacks her pussy hard, a sticky string of her wetness clings to her fingers as her hand comes back down for a second smack, sounding wetter this time.

The bipolar sensations are wreaking havoc inside of me. Watching a hot girl, with a perfect ass—the smell of her arousal like a marketable air freshener, invading me, inserting her fingers into her wet hole. While the unfamiliar pain in my ass reminds me that they have stretched me apart like what happens in one of my videos.

I don't know their exact purpose for doing it and that possibly makes it even more terrifying than knowing... I think.

"You guys, let's just call this whole thing off, let me down." Hearing the panic tone in my own voice cements a certainty into the situation, solidifying the foundation of a fear that seems to grow bigger by every second.

"Ok Fiona, get ready, I'm making the incision now." The clacking from the laptop keys remind me I'm on full display for a bunch of sick fucking women.

"*Incision*!?" My heart runs wild.

Fiona speaks up, belittling me, "don't worry, Wesley, in a minute, you're going to have a big 'ol dick for me.

You'll get to fuck me until I'm so raw, just like *you* wanted."

"You can't get me hard while doing all this, just let me down and I'll get my head in the game. Then we can do whatever you have in mind." I'm begging Fiona, she seems to be the leader in all of this. "Ask the audience, maybe they'd like that more." Even I nearly laugh at my hopefulness.

"Girls?" she says, polling the audience.

The responses she gets back must not be in my favor, they all laugh.

"Resounding no. Sorry, Wesley. What I have in mind *is* happening. I want your *big* dick to fuck me raw. So, I'm having the girls back there open up your asshole, then, that thin layer of flesh separating your dick from said hole, well, Casey is going to make an incision three inches long. Then, Brin will go in from your asshole *through* that taint incision, and push that big dildo *into* your cock, like a foot in a sock—a sock-cock, if you will... and you will."

I feel them making the incision before she's even done talking, and it steals my voice, pain holding it hostage.

I try to scream when I see the big red dildo disappear from the table, nearly choking on the dryness in my mouth, nothing comes out. Tears fall, running down my cheeks, as I feel the massive phallus force into my asshole.

The searing pain as it stretches the slit they've made churns my stomach, but nothing is more painful than the pressure I feel in my flaccid dick as the girl's shove and stretch me until the dildo is sheathed by my cock.

Risking what sanity I have left, I feel compelled to look down and see what they've done.

Shock and nausea take over at the sight of my cartoon dick and I dry heave until I'm dizzy. My head feels fuzzy and I pass out.

***

"He's really holding up well, the last boy was such a mess by this time," I hear one of them saying, and I wish I was still out—or dead.

"Yeah good thing he didn't have the seafood platter like the super-fat-fuck did when he came to kill Casey."

"You guys are dicks for even bringing it up! You know I hate barf, and now I can't even eat sushi without remembering it all over me." Casey makes gagging sounds so realistic; it makes me nauseous myself.

I finally come to, with pain more severe than words can describe. My ass is burning, and my dick feels like I'm trying to squeeze... *another* fucking dick out of it, this one, three times bigger than my own, impregnating it.

"Fuck me, Wesley," Fiona is saying, and I realize the other girls are thrusting me into her, one on either leg, swinging me. "You want to fuck me until I'm raw, huh?"

She taunts me in between moans of pleasure; I have no time to figure out how to handle it. The back and forth motion bringing on the worst bout of seasickness. My dick has no sensation anymore, but the pressure is enough to turn my stomach and twist my equilibrium.

"Oh, no you don't, Wesley." She moves quickly away from me before the next heave happens, but as quick as it appeared, the nausea is gone. As long as I'm not rocking, it subsides.

The ability to breathe, and somewhat center myself, is a welcome distraction for now. But not seeing any of the women makes me paranoid and nervous.

Turning in both directions, as far as I can, lends me nothing in the way of relief. I hear chatter as they entertain their subscribers.

As soon as Brin, the dark-haired nightmare woman, shows herself, I wish to fuck she hadn't.

Mentally willing myself to weigh more so I can tear free is my last defense. She has a wicked looking whip, like Indiana Jones—but not nearly as innocuous looking. The way she cracks it in front of me, barely missing the tip of my nose, tells me she's no stranger to using it.

Without warning, or verbal threat, she cracks it again, this time ringing a vicious scream from deep inside me. The pain from my back ripping apart makes me forget every other thing I've *ever* felt. Shove more dicks inside of my ass and through my dick, but *never* hit me like that again.

Holy fuck!

She seems to appreciate her handy work, striking quicker than I can prepare for, and then another. The skin on my back opens up, I feel the trickles of blood. One last flick from her wrist and then a giggle from the girls as I lose my bladder. I openly cry, heaving sobs from pain I didn't think possible to live through.

"It's coming out his ass!" Fiona shrieks, clapping her hands and bouncing. "Ass pisser!"

The laughter from the computer makes me wish I was dead. It's like 4th grade, and the girls are just assholes for no reason. Chanting of my new nickname embarrasses me further—*annoying*.

"Ass pisser..."

"*Gross*, Wesley," Casey mocks, and being such an incognito mean-girl, it actually bothers me more coming from her.

She dips under me to take the monster cock between both of her hands. The sensation is mild, but nothing like I'm used to, then she jacks it off. Her small hands making it look even larger than the forearm-size it is, and makes me wonder if it was painful for Fiona to have inside of her. I hope it was, but that doesn't make me feel any better.

"I want a shot at this," instead of Casey getting to her hands and knees, the blonde wraps her arms around my neck and leaps, locking her legs around my hips, her big fake tits pressed into my chest.

"Get him inside me." The other two help her with her request. "Oh, my god, you're so big, Wesley." Wildly, she works herself against me, getting loud and seemingly enjoying this.

I am just relieved that she doesn't need the other ones to move me, that was horrible. She keeps her head back awkwardly, maybe it's to keep my mouth away from her neck so I don't bite her fucking head off, I can't be sure. The other girls are holding my arms back, if they're thinking it's saving me from choking her, it's pointless. I'd lost control of them long ago when the sensation of them ran away.

She fucks herself into an orgasm, the sight of it confirms that I might have never actually succeeded in giving one before. Childishly, I get annoyed at that.

She slows, exhausted, and flops on top of the mattress below, bouncing as her body hits it. Her pussy is red rimmed and raw looking.

I ask again to be let go. But I suppose, even if they did let me go, which I'm sure is not a real option, it may not even be a worthwhile life in my future. My dick will never be the same. It will never be functional, and I almost wish for death—knowing I'll never be whole again.

I can't even mourn that for long though, because the whispers have taught me that horrible things are coming, and this time is no different.

Naively, I thought keeping an eye on one would have me informed, but while Casey lain there recovering, the other girls were conspiring. Bringing with them the sick fucking bitches watching the stream. Together making the most frightening fucking force ever.

I don't know what they are doing, but I feel the pressure as they pull the dildo out of me. It's not as relieving as I thought it would be. I look at my stretched and empty dick, long enough to catch a glimpse, but I can't lose what sanity I have remaining, so I look away before I cry again, trying to scrub that from my mind.

Oh, god, they've turned me into an empty sock puppet.

Held back tears fall, as I try to fight them back again.

The dildo doesn't come all the way out of my ass though, I feel them pushing it further inside my butthole, instead. I thought it had hurt being stretched, but it feels so much worse having them shove it deeper. I try to fight the intrusion to no avail. The bright red dong is as big as an arm, I've never had anything but a finger in my butt, and I'm not prepared for how to handle this.

What do the men in porn tell women to do when taking their dicks? To breathe? I can't fucking *breathe*!

I'm screaming, I realize, and the audience is loving it. Smiley faces and heart eyes floating up on the screen like children's escaped balloons.

No lube, nothing, just two girls shoving a fist-sized cock up my butt. It takes my breath away and brings burning tears to my eyes. Again.

"You want to fuck all my holes, Wesley?" Fiona taunts.

And then it dawns on me, they asked what I wanted to do to the girl during my application questionnaire. These bitches are going to do it all to me. I try to recall how in depth I got with my claims and aspirations.

Then, horrified, I remember the amputation, and I lose it. I try to struggle again, clenching my ass in vain. The dong feels so large, like it might exit through my face, as I try to push it out, birth it back into the world where it isn't inside of me.

The girls don't stop, they rape me with a fierce aggression. Shoving hard, heaving in tandem, like they are trying to break down a castle gate.

The sound of nails on the keyboard making me want to lash-out. Casey grabs hold of her boobs, perfect surgical symmetry, and massages them, "Oh, Wesley, are you having as much fun as we are? You're being such a good boy," she mocks.

"Fuck you!" I can't help but blurt out, fuck this.

"Oh, fuck me, Wesley? How about, instead, fuck you?" Grabbing the dangling skin that is my dick now, Casey makes one quick snip with the scissors and shows me my stretched-out dick free of my body, flapping in her hand.

"You mean with this thing?" Her laughter is heart wrenching. Swinging it around like a single wet sock, it makes me sick, this time I do hurl.

"It makes me sick, too. You were always a limp dick; it just took us to show *you* what you really are."

Leaning back, Casey crudely smacks her pussy with it, blood stains her pink flesh and she continues. Then, she takes it by the head, I can't help but look horrified, and puts it in her mouth, slurping it up like a spaghetti noodle.

"Getting off on killing innocent women is vile and unforgivable." She tongues the tip and I cringe.

Her hand working its way inside until she wears it like a glove. "How about you fuck yourself, literally?" Turning her head to the screen, Casey asks if anyone has any special requests.

"I do." I hear a small voice break the pause. "I have a request for forty-grand guy."

I have to look at the screen, focus on the voice, see who it belongs to.

"Go ahead, chicky, what should I do?"

"S-S-Steph?" I studder.

"Hey Wesley," she waves like a child spotting her mother in a crowd. Ignoring me, she tells Casey her request. "Sock fuck him hard, he deserves it, fuckin' liar, scum!" Steph shouts.

She never shouts.

The girls laugh, Fiona ooooooo-ing like some secret has just been revealed. "The wife has spoken!" she announces with her finger in the air.

I lose sight of Casey as she moves behind me, I just know she is going to put my dick inside my ass. And the sobs begin to choke me. I was just barely off about the size of the dong, it is smaller, only slightly, than a forearm. She punches my insides, I swear I can feel it inside my chest, it's impossible to catch my breath, I feel the pounding in my head as the blood pulses though my wounds.

With an abrupt quickness, she appears in front of me, the bloodied dick-condom on her arm, proudly shown to me in crudeness.

Then Brin asks the screen once more for requests, and I pray, like I never have, that they all say nothing, and that even this has already gone too far. That the audience might encourage the women to let me go.

The next best thing happens... silence. No more additional things added to my already-long-list of torture.

Casey doesn't seem to care whether there was a response. She removes my dick skin inside-out, and flops it onto the floor like a surgical glove, and that, somehow, is what does me in. I scream for help until my throat feels bloody, and then I continue, praying Stephanie has had a change of heart, it's only money, after all.

I can't die like this; I can't be immortalized for all the internet freaks to get off to. Especially now that I know the internet freaks are a bunch of crazy-ass fucking women.

I can't escape, I'm a turtle stuck upside-down in his shell, there is no hope for me. No help, no rationalizing with these heartless and callous women.

Somehow it pisses me off right now, that I learned my costly snuff films were faked, and that this, *oh my fucking god, this* is real.

The planning that had gone into this is wild. They'd used that screenname for years, three at least. They had provided me with most of my collection—my *fake* collection. My mind loses hope. All I have now is the wish that they make this quick. That I can finally just die. I focus on that, the darkness of death and hope it's here soon.

And a little part of me wishes I had talked to Steph about all this after all, another part wishing she'd burn in a fiery car accident for letting them do this to me.

Would karma help me out, surely, they've done more wrong than I?

Three

I think, for a second, what it might take for me to appear so boring that they all forget about me and slink back in to the dark hellholes from whence they've spawned, losing all interest in me, and that they'll call it quits. I mean, really, what else could they do to me?

Too soon, I learn the answer.

A girl at either of my arms, spreading them wide, and then Fiona busying herself at each. I can't see from this angle, but I know there's a ligature just under each of my arm pits. My limbs, down to my fingers, which I thought were already numb, lose every ounce of sensation after tightening. A loud whirring in my ears as the blood pumps harder to break the damn.

"Wesley, you said something about wanting to hack off my limbs. You're a real sicko. I'm sure the ladies would all *love* to see you lose yours, next to the sock fuck, this is their favorite. A real brutal bunch, they are," Fiona mocks me with her disdainful eyes.

She lifts the cord and walks it over to the post at the end of the room, and then does the same to the other side. She moves with no quickness at all, which I both hate, and appreciate.

All three girls appear in front of me, relief doesn't even begin to flourish before I feel a tugging. Then a stronger pull. The razor sharpness of something cutting into my biceps deeply, scoring my flesh. The pain intensifies as the pull continues.

Tearing my skin and muscle from the bone, both my arms fall heavy to the ground, empty of the bones that are still attached to me. The sight of my inside-out flesh brings a new sensation along my body—a wave of dread, felt like tickling energy, envelopes me, alighting the frenzy of fear.

I see both of my arms lying on the ground. The girls, Brin and Casey, come over to grab me by my flesh naked wrists. Fiona left holding a webcam to show me off.

"The secret to amputation, is removing the flesh first, and then," Fiona says, wrenching my arm, a cracking sound rings through my body, shocking my ears, "remove it at the joint, like a rotisserie chicken."

Through my hazy, shock-filled, eyes, I see the strange gleeful smile on her lips. I have to turn away before it resonates too deeply that it could have been on my face, for her to see while I toyed with her, if roles had remained the same. I'm thinking now, it may be too terrible to inflict on another human. And a sliver of regret splinters inside me, cutting inside my chest.

I'm not awake for the second break. If there was anything else that happened in the last few minutes of peaceful unconsciousness, I don't know that either, I realize I had lost consciousness again only when I awaken.

I've been lowered atop the mattress and onto my back. I try to make a run for it. That mostly happens mentally, as no part of my body will listen to instructions my brain shouts at them.

"Wesley, do you remember what else you wanted to do to me?" Fiona sits next to me, whispering into my ear, oddly seductive.

"I'm sorry," I say, actually meaning it. I hadn't weighed the value of life before now—before it was mine on the scale.

"I know that, silly," she laughs. "I also know you *love* a good money shot," her excitement is more chilling now.

"Sick fucking *bitches*!" I shout, knowing after it's out, that it doesn't insult them, it doesn't even fuel them, it just makes them giggle—those horrible twinkling sounds that I used to think made such a beautiful call to those who heard. A sound of flirty sexuality that had many a time swollen me hard. Now, sending revulsion throughout my body, instead.

Casey walks over and brusquely slices a box cutter down the center of my chest, the blood trickles from it, pooling on either side of me. Sliding her finger inside of it, the feel of her dirty digit mangling the cut, opening it wider.

I can only hope that this is it, let me die now.

All three girls take standing positions above me, straddling their legs across me, and begin rubbing themselves. The thought of them able to get off on this is sickening, hypocrisy be *damned*. "You wanted to come inside my open wounds, remember?" Fiona taunts.

Working in unison, they all rub quickly, moaning loudly—above the level porn should be heard, it's too much. A hot liquid shoots from Brin's pussy, spraying my chest and face. The burning sting inside the cut along my chest feels like salt and fire.

Casey comes next, quivering as she inserts her finger inside her pussy and then traces it through my yawning wound, bringing it back to her mouth to suck the finger as I look on, mouth agape, I'm both horrified and disgusted.

Fiona plops down, a leg on either side of my chest, sliding along the wetness left behind by the other two, grinding her pussy against me like a crude, makeshift slip and slide. Her eyes hood, her face contorts as she comes on me, splashing the mingling fluid about, reminiscent of a young girl at a pool party, coyly playing around.

And then all three of them produce short bladed knives, stabbing into me, striking hard and fast until I don't feel it anymore, I don't feel anything at all.

***

"Alright, ladies, you know to keep our secrets. It's no fun to let the boys in on this. If you want to sponsor a snuff, shoot us a link to his profile."

"Donate to Killstreme if you want to continue to be a member and keep up-to-date with all the cool fucking shit we do," Brin says to the camera as we end the night. Zooming in to the aftermath of poor Wesley.

four

"Hey mom, how come you're up so early?" I ask.

"Had a scratchy throat, just up for a glass of water. Do you want breakfast?"

"No, thank you. I'm beat, long night at work."

"I'm proud of you Fiona, I'm sure you're doing great things."

I am actually having a hard time keeping upright. My entire body feels like it's been run over and the *last* thing I want is to take another step on this fucking toe.

I can't tell her what the Killstreme girls and I do, but I think we *are* doing great things. "I am, mom. Goodnight."

***

Lunch with the girls for the recap is pretty norm. We like to go over the feedback from viewers. It's important that we listen to them and give them what they want to see.

Even though I started this with Brin, bringing Casey in a few months later—we felt like the world was missing something. And that something was us—it feels necessary to include the subscribers in a few of the aspects. Some even playing the actresses in some pretty horrific videos to target the audience we like to keep close—enemies and all that.

Thinking that, although, women don't *generally* like this kind of stuff, snuff, brutality, and just plain horrible things, there had to be *some* that thought like us. That we could cater to the few and maybe do something about our money situations with it.

The popularity of Killstreme among our women viewers only took half a year to grow beyond what any other company like ours ever had—mainstream or underground.

We are who everyone goes to for their filth, but only women know it's us who run Killstreme. Be it your typical female victim snuff, hardcore, brutal... anything you need to hide on your browser, that's us.

We have the entire market in our pocket, and production spares no expense when it comes to the finished product.

"Did you see the reactions we got when we showed Bella to Wesley?" Brin says, "the bitches *loved* it! I'm thinking we could venture into a revenge thing and get even bigger. Cheaters, sickos, all of them."

Dipping my chip into the guac, I say to her, "that's brilliant, I'm glad I caught her in the crowd. His eyes almost popped out of his head seeing her. His fucking world *crumbled*. It was great."

Casey leans forward, "and then his *wife*! It just wasn't his night." She laughs, she loves when karma helps us out.

"I have Baldwin coming in for a gig. We need Maranda to come in and do a scene with him. The boys are getting restless on the dark, we gotta give them another release. I'll get everything ready for this week. We need the loft open for filming," I tell them both.

"Sounds good. I'll let everyone know to be ready for the call," Brin says.

"Since we are talking about the revenge thing being an option, I may have a guy. My cousin is with a major douche. Could we talk to her and see if she'd be interested in getting free of him?" Casey asks, still feeling like the last girl to join the club, even though it's been years now.

"Is she a subscriber?" I ask.

"Top tier."

"Get her in touch with me. I'll talk to her, see what we could do."

"Thanks, Fi."

"Now that business is all handled, can we start the margaritas, please. I'm fucking wrecked from last night," Brin says, laughing as she indicates she wants the waitress to stop over.

"Hell yea, job well done, girls."

Thank you for reading. You, reader, are appreciated.

Thank you.